Another Way to Climb a Tree

Liz Garton Scanlon

Pictures by

Hadley Hooper

A NEAL PORTER BOOK
ROARING BROOK PRESS
NEW YORK

Lulu climbs
the tallest trees
in the neighborhood,

the ones with the widest branches,

the biggest knots, and the stickiest sap.

Lulu climbs the trees
that trap cats

and the trees
that catch kites

and
the
trees
that
other
kids
won't
climb.

Lulu even climbs
the trees other kids
fall out of.

When Lulu sees
a climbing tree,

she's here,

and then she's gone,
just like that.

When Lulu's sick,
the birds miss her . . .
so do the branches.

When Lulu's sick,
she looks out her window
at the trees missing her

and she misses them right back.

Lulu grows pale
and quiet.

The birds
stop singing
and the branches bend.

Nobody climbs the trees
but the sun,

bit by bright
warm
bit.

Lulu's jealous.

The sun spends nearly
the whole day there,

climbing and
reaching
and resting.

And then at night,

the moon does
the very same thing.

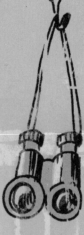

Lulu turns her back
on the bright branches.

But there—there it is,
waiting, on her wall—
the tallest, widest, biggest tree of all.

And Lulu, with her fingertips,
climbs that tree,

bit by bright
warm
bit.

She reaches and swings and
twists and hides.
She's here . . .

and then she's gone,
just like that.

For Audrey, climbing and reaching —L.G.S.

For H. LuLu W. —H.H.

Text copyright © 2017 by Liz Garton Scanlon
Illustrations copyright © 2017 by Hadley Hooper
A Neal Porter Book
Published by Roaring Brook Press
Roaring Brook Press is a division of Holtzbrinck Publishing
Holdings Limited Partnership
175 Fifth Avenue, New York, New York 10010
The art for this book was created using traditional art materials and printmaking techniques
that were scanned in and assembled in Photoshop.
mackids.com

Library of Congress Cataloging-in-Publication Data

Names: Scanlon, Elizabeth Garton, author. | Hooper, Hadley, illustrator.
Title: Another way to climb a tree / Liz Garton Scanlon ; illustrated by
Hadley Hooper.
Description: First edition. | New York : Roaring Brook Press, 2017. | "A Neal
Porter book." | Summary: "When Lulu's feeling well, she climbs every tree
in sight. But when Lulu's sick, all she has is her imagination and a
shadow"— Provided by publisher.
Identifiers: LCCN 2016039718 | ISBN 9781626723528 (hardback)
Subjects: | CYAC: Tree climbing—Fiction. | Trees—Fiction. |
Imagination—Fiction. | BISAC: JUVENILE FICTION / Imagination & Play. |
JUVENILE FICTION / Lifestyles / Country Life. | JUVENILE FICTION / Health
& Daily Living / General.
Classification: LCC PZ7.S2798 An 2017 | DDC [E]—dc23
LC record available at https://lccn.loc.gov/2016039718

Our books may be purchased in bulk for promotional, educational, or business use. Please
contact your local bookseller or the Macmillan Corporate and Premium Sales Department
at (800) 221-7945 ext. 5442 or by e-mail at MacmillanSpecialMarkets@macmillan.com.

First edition 2017
Printed in China by RR Donnelley Asia Printing Solutions Ltd., Dongguan City, Guangdong Province
2   4   6   8   10   9   7   5   3   1